To:

From:

Little Linus, Little Linus,
off we go on a grand ride.
It'll be a great adventure,
stay close by my side!

Little Linus, Little Linus,
we'll start by the pond.

Please bring my hat,
please bring my wand.

Little Linus, Little Linus,
we'll swing from the trees.

We'll climb
tall mountains.

We'll swim
in the seas.

Little Linus, Little Linus,
we'll make new friends.

We'll escape
from enemies.

We'll glide
in the winds.

Little Linus, Little Linus,
we'll eat snacks all day.

We'll sleep
all afternoon.

Under the stars
we'll play.

Little Linus, Little Linus,
I must share a secret.
Hold it close to your heart,
and promise to keep it.

Little Linus, Little Linus,
our adventure will end.
You'll grow big and strong.
Your own journey will begin.

Little Linus, Little Linus,
my dreams came true.

My greatest adventures
are just memories...
memories of you.

To be continued...

First edition July 2020

ISBN 978-1-7351705-6-5 (hardback)
ISBN 978-1-7351705-7-2 (paperback)
ISBN 978-1-7351705-8-9 (ebook)

www.linusthewizard.com